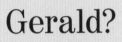

Worms
are slimy.

Worms like
to wiggle.

And you cannot
tell their tops from
their bottoms!

Oh, look! Flowers!

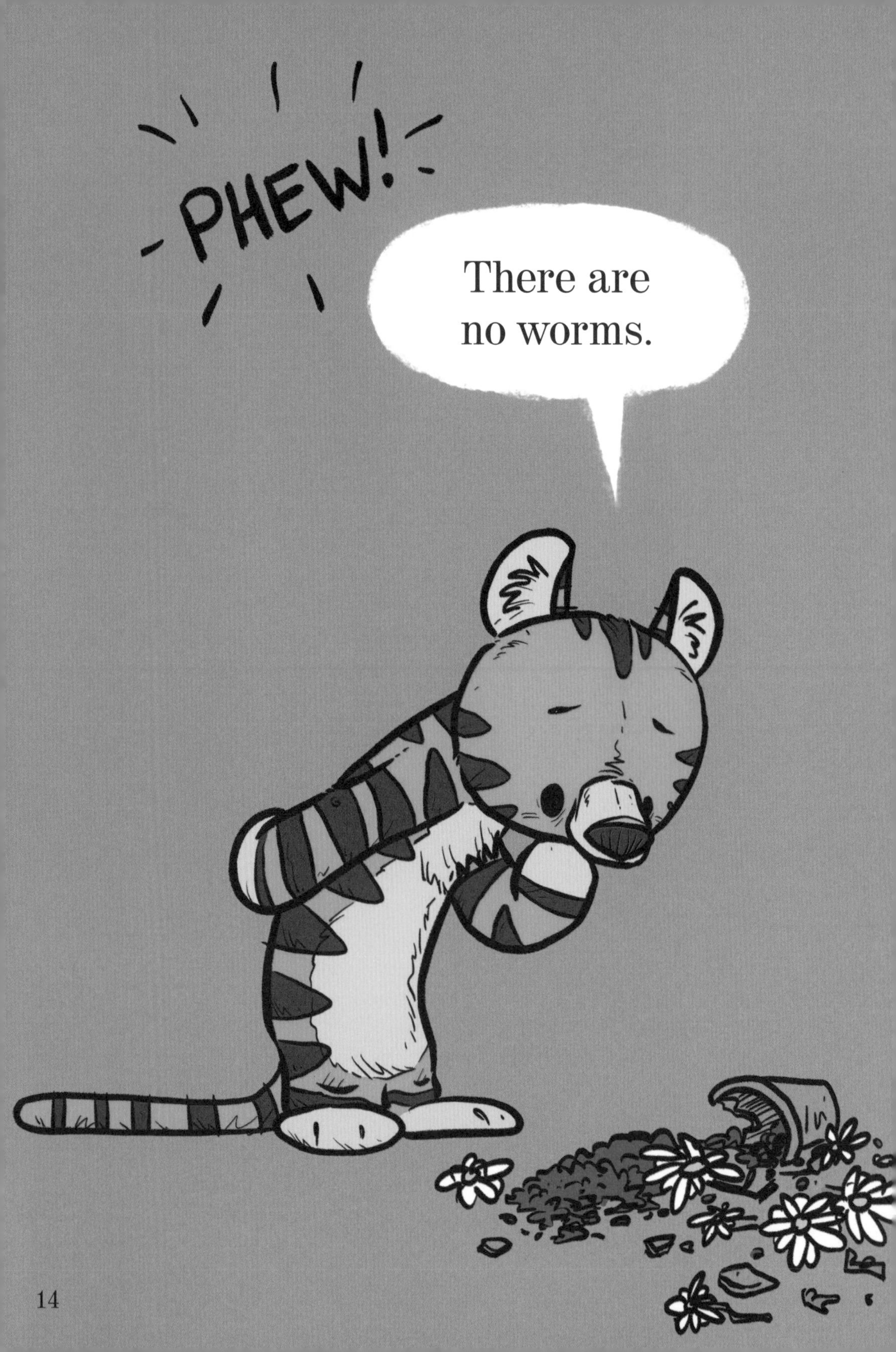
PHEW!
There are no worms.

... sigh ...

But I did break the flowerpot.

...GULP!...

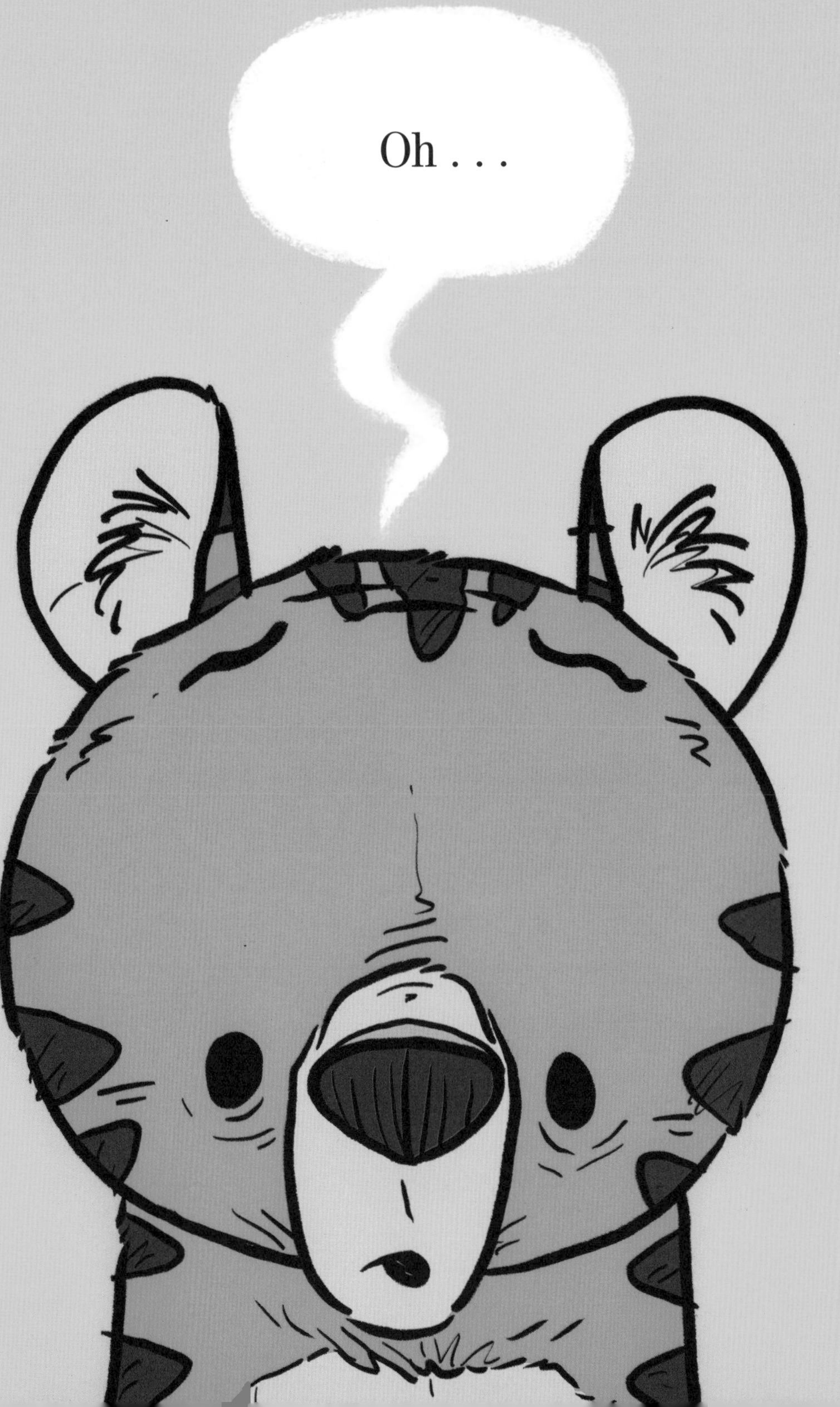
Oh . . .

Worms ruin
everything.

Thanks a lot, WORMS!

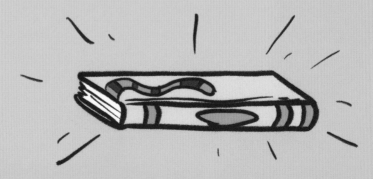

OH NO!

GULP!

What if it is
a book about . . .

...WOOOOOO

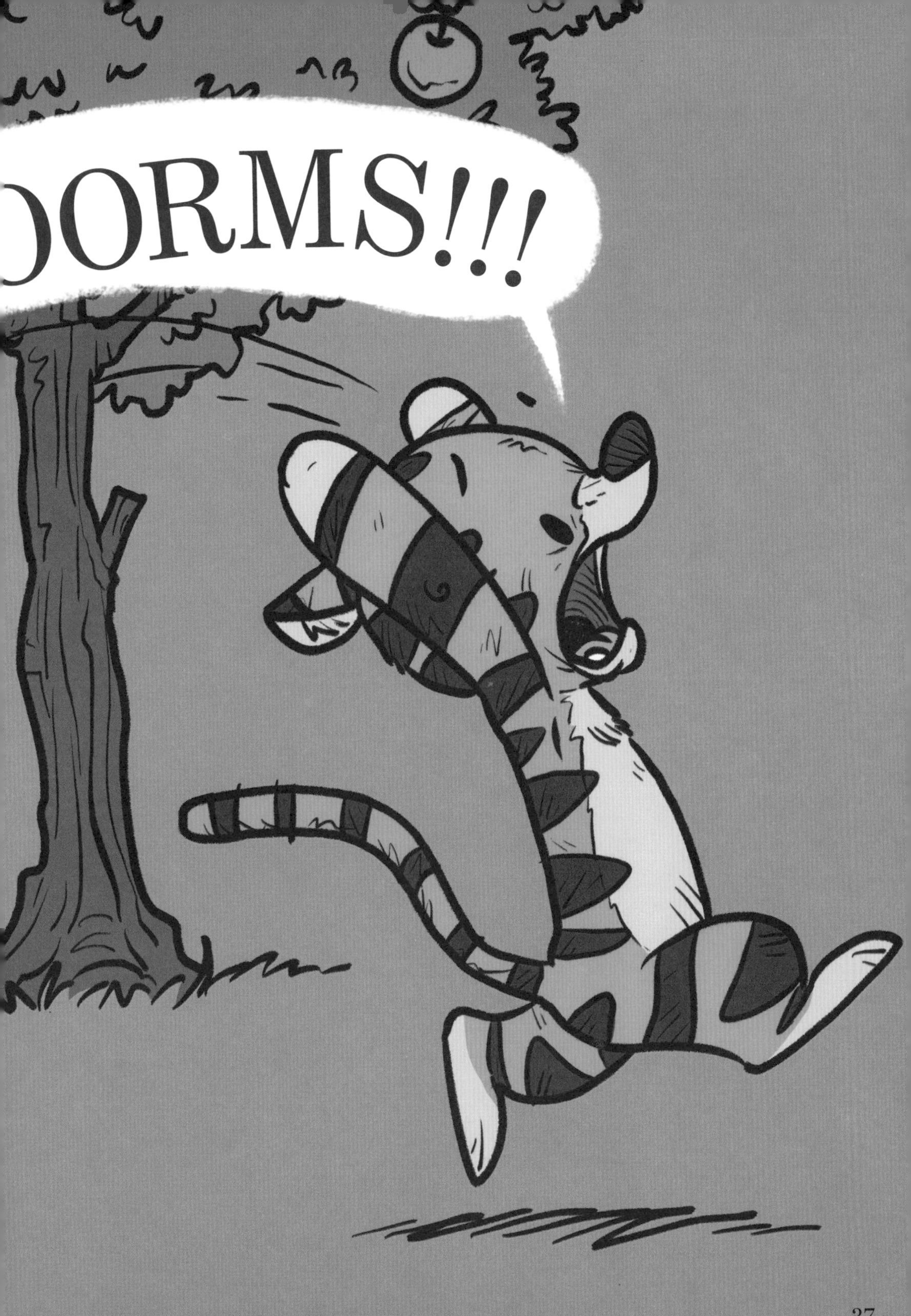
ORMS!!!

Tigers are furry.

Tigers like to walk.

And you can tell their tops from their bottoms!

41

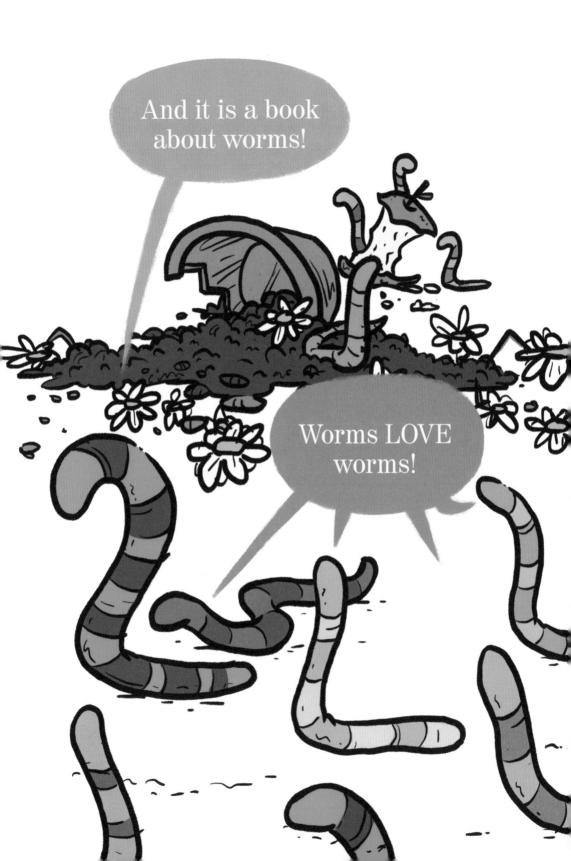

48

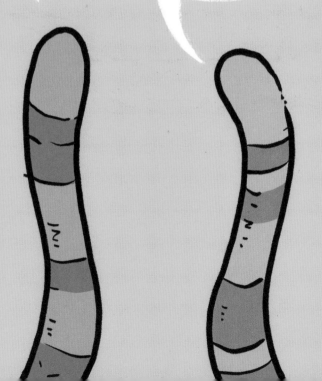

We learned SO MUCH! And now...

Worms LOVE tigers!

That nice tiger
left us dirt,
an apple,
and a book.

49

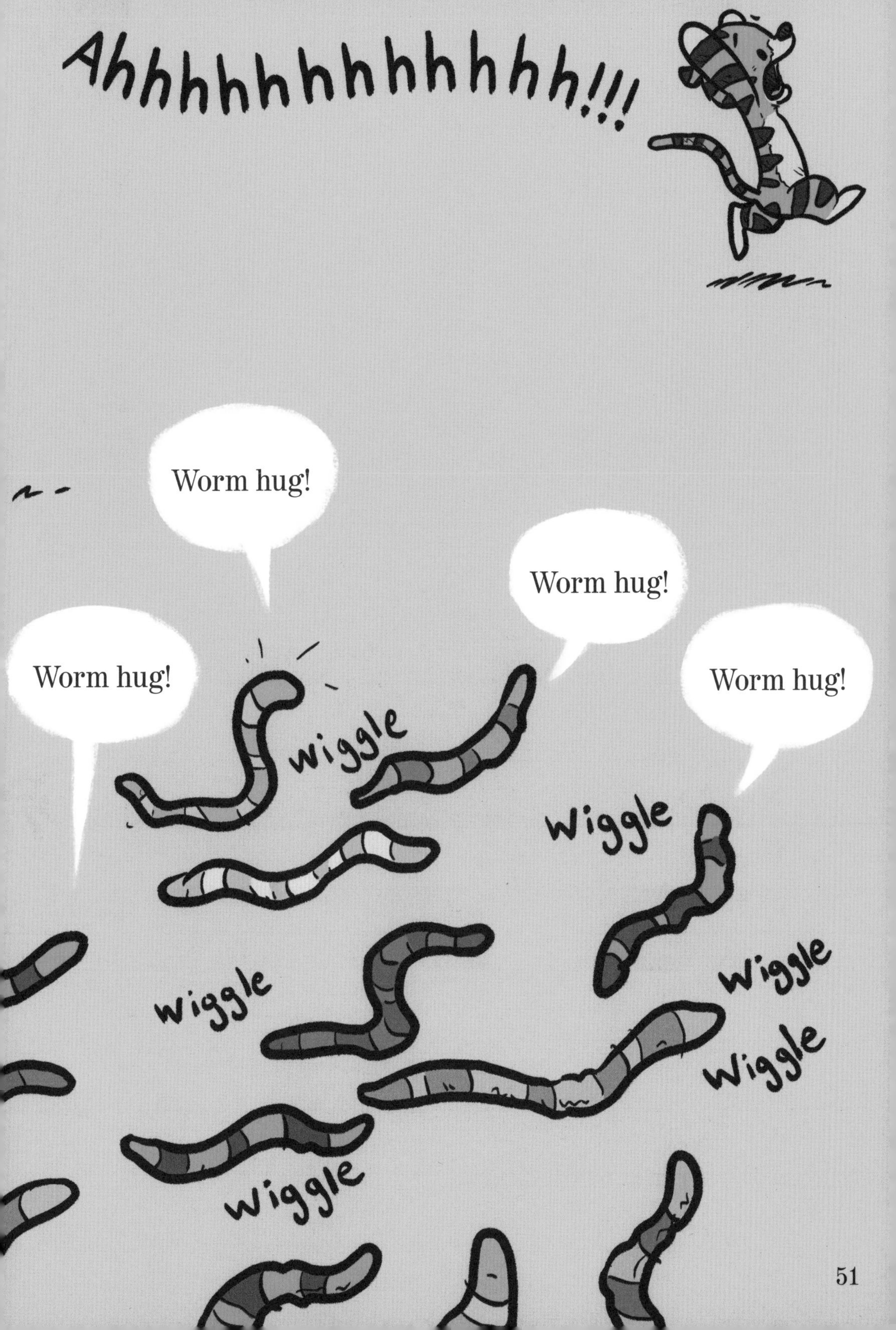
Ahhhhhhhhhhhh!!!
Worm hug!
Worm hug!
Worm hug!
Worm hug!
wiggle
wiggle
wiggle
wiggle
wiggle
wiggle

For Mo
—R.T.H.

First Edition, May 2020 • 1 3 5 7 9 10 8 6 4 2 • FAC-029191-20024 • Printed in Malaysia

This book is set in Century 725/Monotype; Grilled Cheese BTN/Fontbros, with hand-lettering by Ryan T. Higgins

Library of Congress Cataloging-in-Publication Data

Names: Willems, Mo, author, illustrator. • Higgins, Ryan T., author,
illustrator. • Title: What about worms!? / by [Mo Willems and] Ryan T. Higgins.
Description: First edition. • New York : Hyperion Books for Children, 2020. •
Series: Elephant & Piggie like reading! ; [7] • Summary: Tiger unwittingly
helps some worms overcome their fear of tigers with a well-placed,
informative book, but will a wormy hug aid a fearful Tiger?
Identifiers: LCCN 2019019930 • ISBN 9781368045735 (paper over board)
Subjects: • CYAC: Fear—Fiction. • Tiger—Fiction. • Worms—Fiction.
Classification: LCC PZ7.W65535 Wg 2020 • DDC [E]—dc23
LC record available at https://lccn.loc.gov/2019019930

Reinforced binding

Visit hyperionbooksforchildren.com
and pigeonpresents.com